WAH-A-WAH-WAH!

JINGLE, SHA-JANGLE!

PING, TING-A-LING!

DOODLE, DOODLE, DOOT!

BOOM, DADA, BOOM!

CLANG-CLANG, SHA-BANG!

VRING, VREE-OH-RING!

TWEE-OH-EE, OH

ROOT-A-TO ,TOOT!

To John and Vicki,
for all you do

*To Ariella May and her parents*

Let every creature
praise his holy name.
Psalm 145:21

*I read this book many times*
*with my grandchildren!*
*May it bless you*
*and our Lord*

*Love, Auntie Jacque Pasko*
*May 2015*

The Standard Publishing Company, Cincinnati, Ohio
A division of Standex International Corporation
© 1993 by The Standard Publishing Company
All rights reserved.
Printed in the United States of America
00 99 98 97 96 95 94 93    5 4 3 2 1

Library of Congress Catalog Card Number 92-32817
ISBN 0-7847-0036-2
Cataloging-in-Publication data available
Designed by Coleen Davis

# ALEXANDER'S

## PRAISE TIME BAND

written by Diane Stortz
illustrated by Norma Garris

LITTLE DEER
B·O·O·K·S
PSALM 42:1

Standard Publishing
Cincinnati, Ohio

with his shiny french horn.

# A-WAH-WAH!

But Alexander was tired of playing and praising all by himself.
"I want to play in a band," he said, "a special band—
a Praise Time Band!"
So he set off to find some friends
to play in his Praise Time Band.

Near a cluster of banana plants, Alexander heard a sound. Mr. Monkey was playing his tambourine.

JINGLE,

"That's a very fine sound," said Alexander.
"Thank you," said Mr. Monkey. "But I am growing tired of playing and praising all by myself."
"Then come and join my Praise Time Band!" said Alexander.
With a jingle, sha-jangle! Mr. Monkey scrambled down from the banana plant, and Alexander and Mr. Monkey marched through the jungle, playing and praising God together.

SHA-JANGLE!

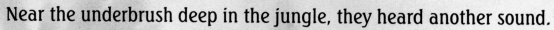

Near the underbrush deep in the jungle, they heard another sound.

BOOM, DADA, BOOM!

Mr. Tiger was playing his drum.
"That's a very fine sound," said Alexander.
"Thank you," said Mr. Tiger. "But I am growing tired
of playing and praising all by myself."

"Then come and join my Praise Time Band!" said Alexander.
With a boom, dada, boom! Mr. Tiger bounced to the back
of the line, and all the animals marched through the
jungle, playing and praising God together.

Mr. Elephant was playing his cymbals.
"That's a very fine sound," said Alexander.
"Thank you," said Mr. Elephant. "But I am growing tired of playing and praising all by myself."

"Then come and join my Praise Time Band!" said Alexander. With a clang, clang, sha-bang! Mr. Elephant lumbered into the line, and all the animals marched and played and praised God together—right out of the jungle and into the forest.

In the forest, they heard another sound.
Mr. Fox was playing his clarinet.

DOODLE,
DOODLE,
DOOT!

"That's a very fine sound,"
said Alexander.
"Thank you," said Mr. Fox. "But
I am growing tired of playing
and praising all by myself."
"Then come and join my Praise
Time Band!" said Alexander.
Mr. Fox sauntered into the line
with a doodle, doodle, doot!
And all the animals marched
through the forest, playing
and praising God together.

Near a cave in the mountain,
the animals heard another sound.
Mrs. Bear was playing her flute.

TWEE-OH-EE,

"That's a very fine
sound," said Alexander.

**OH-EE!**

"Thank you," said Mrs. Bear. "But I am growing tired of playing and praising all by myself."

"Then come and join my Praise Time Band!" said Alexander.

With a twee-oh-ee, oh-ee! Mrs. Bear shuffled into place, and all the animals marched through the forest, playing and praising God together.

Under the giant oak tree,
they heard another sound.
Mr. Squirrel was playing his trumpet.

ROOT-
A-TOOT, TOOT!

"That's a very fine sound," said Alexander.
"Thank you," said Mr. Squirrel. "But I am growing tired
of playing and praising all by myself."

"Then come and join
my Praise Time Band!"
said Alexander.

With a root-a-toot, toot! Mr. Squirrel scurried down from
the tree, and all the animals marched and played and
praised God together—right out of the forest and into the
countryside.

Near the meadow, they heard another sound.
Mr. Rabbit was playing his violin.

VRING, VREE-OH-

"That's a very fine sound," said Alexander.
"Thank you," said Mr. Rabbit. "But I am growing tired of
playing and praising all by myself."

RING!

"Then come and join my Praise Time Band!" said Alexander. With a vring, vree-oh-ring! Mr. Rabbit hopped into place and all the animals marched through the countryside, playing and praising God together.

When they came to the pond, they heard another sound. Mrs. Duck was playing her triangle.

PING,

# TING-A-LING!

"That's a very fine sound," said Alexander.
"Thank you," said Mr. Duck. "But I am growing tired of playing and praising all by myself."
"Then come and join my Praise Time Band!" said Alexander. With a ping, ting-a-ling! Mrs. Duck waddled into the line, and all the animals marched and played and praised God together—right out of the countryside and into the town.

And the people in the town heard a sound!

Children came to the windows and stood in the doorways and joined the parade. They clapped their hands . . .

and danced and waved as the animals played and praised God together, marching through the town.

Music floated softly on a breeze
as Alexander's Praise Time Band marched away.
"Good-bye! Good-bye!" the children called.
"Please come back soon!"

And they did!

# INSTRUMENTS YOU CAN MAKE

## RHYTHM STICKS

Cut half-inch dowels into 12" lengths. Sand the ends smooth. Use in pairs.

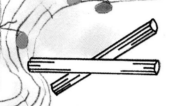

## SAND BLOCKS

Start with smooth wooden blocks, about 5" x 3". Tack or glue strips of coarse sandpaper over the ends and one long side of each block. Add knobs to opposite sides for handles.

## SHAKERS

Fill small metal containers (such as spice cans) with seeds or beans. Glue and tape containers securely shut, and cover the containers with adhesive-backed plastic.

## DRUM

Remove both ends of a three-pound coffee can. Cover can with adhesive-backed plastic. Glue a plastic lid over each end. Beat the drum with hands or dowel sticks.

# PRAISE HIM, PRAISE HIM

—unknown

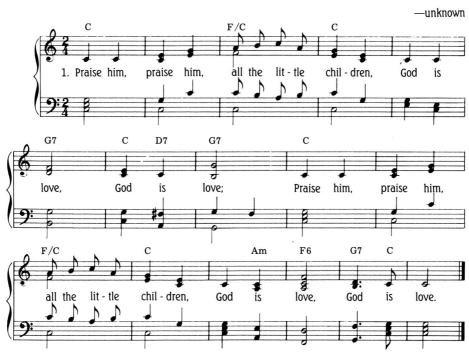

1. Praise him, praise him, all the lit-tle chil-dren, God is love, God is love; Praise him, praise him, all the lit-tle chil-dren, God is love, God is love.

2. Love him   3. Thank him

WAH-A-WAH-WAH!
JINGLE, SHA-JANGLE!
BOOM, DADA, BOOM!
PING,
TING-A-LING!
DOODLE, DOODLE, DOOT!
TWEE-
OH-EE, OH-EE!
CLANG-CLANG,
SHA-BANG!
VRING, VREE-OH-RING!
ROOT-
A-TOOT, TOOT!